Monica
the Marshmallow
Fairy

To Aleka, with love

Special thanks to Rachel Elliot

All rights reserved. Published by Scholastic Inc., *Publishers since 1920.* SCHOLASTIC and associated logos are trademarks and/or registered trademarks of Scholastic Inc. RAINBOW MAGIC is a trademark of Rainbow Magic Limited. Reg. U.S. Patent & Trademark Office and other countries. HIT and the HIT logo are trademarks of HIT Entertainment Limited.

First published in the United Kingdom in 2017 by Orchard U.K., Carmelite House, 50 Victoria Embankment, London EC4Y 0DZ.

ISBN 978-1-338-20718-7

10 9 8 7 6 5 4 3 2 1   18 19 20 21 22

Printed in the U.S.A.   40
First printing 2018

Monica the Marshmallow Fairy

by Daisy Meadows

SCHOLASTIC INC.

Jack Frost's Ice Castle

Animal Shelter

Community Center

Children's Hospital

Give me candy! Give me sweets!
Give me sticky, chewy treats!
Lollipops and fudge so yummy—
Bring them here to fill my tummy.

Monica, I'll steal from you.
Gabby, Franny, Shelley, too.
I will build a candy shop,
So I can eat until I pop!

Contents

A Magical Invitation   1

Thieves in the Orchard   11

Summer Snow   21

Trouble in the Tree House   31

Smelly Sweets   43

Helping Hands   55

A Magical Invitation

"Welcome back to Wetherbury!" said Kirsty Tate.

Her best friend, Rachel Walker, placed a raspberry-colored suitcase on Kirsty's bed.

"I'm so happy to be here with you for the week!" she said. "I'll unpack my things, and then we can go and play."

As she reached out to open the suitcase, Mrs. Tate came in holding the phone.

"It's your aunt Helen," she told Kirsty.

Kirsty took the phone, and Mrs. Tate left the room. As Kirsty chatted with her aunt, a huge smile lit up her face, and Rachel hopped from foot to foot, longing to know what was being said. Aunt Helen worked at Candy Land, the candy factory outside the village, which Kirsty and Rachel thought just might be the best job in the world.

Kirsty hung up the phone and clapped her hands together.

"Rachel, Aunt Helen's going to be here any minute," she said, brimming with excitement. "She's going to pick us up in the Candy Land van for a special trip."

Rachel squealed, and the girls joined

hands and spun around
in delight.

"Do you think
she's going to
take us to Candy
Land?" Kirsty said.

"If she does, I
wonder if we'll
see the Sugar and
Spice Fairies again," said
Rachel.

She and Kirsty shared a happy smile.
The last time they had seen Aunt Helen,
they had been caught up in a magical
adventure with their fairy friends.
Because they had promised to always
keep the secrets of Fairyland, they
couldn't tell anyone else about their
adventures. It was always wonderful to

be able to talk about magic together.

Just then, Rachel's raspberry-colored suitcase started to glow. The clasps rattled, and then the suitcase burst open and a tiny fairy fluttered out. She was wearing a buttoned denim skirt, a fluffy sweater, and pink sandals, and her shiny brown hair swished around her face.

"Hello, Rachel and Kirsty," she said. "I'm Monica the Marshmallow Fairy."

"It's amazing to meet you," said Kirsty.

"Welcome to Wetherbury . . . but what
are you doing here?"

"I'm one of the Sweet Fairies," said
Monica, perching on the open lid of the
suitcase. "I'm here to take you to the
Candy Factory in Fairyland. The Sweet
Fairies are hoping to speak to you—will
you come?"

The girls exchanged a look of
sheer delight. They had been to the
Candy Factory before, and they knew
that it was a magical place full of
sweet fairy treats.

"Of course," they said together.

"We always love visiting Fairyland,"
Kirsty went on. "And luckily, time always
stops in the human world while we're
there, so we'll be back before Aunt Helen
arrives to pick us up."

"Great! I need you to sit on your bed, please," said Monica, smiling.

Kirsty and Rachel sat down beside the suitcase, and Monica raised her wand. A flurry of tiny pink marshmallows danced around the girls, and they saw fairy dust sparkling as they shrank to fairy size. Their wings unfurled, and Monica fluttered down to join them.

"Hold hands, girls," she said. "Let's go to Fairyland."

There was a sudden, sweet smell, and the tiny marshmallows danced faster and faster, lifting them into the air. Then Kirsty's bedroom disappeared and the swirl of marshmallows slowed down. As the last marshmallows disappeared, they saw that they were standing by the Fairyland Candy Factory—in an orchard of delicious-looking trees.

"Oh, I love it here," said Rachel, clapping her hands together. "I wish our yard had candy growing on the trees."

"And these trees are always growing new treats to enjoy!" said another voice.

Three other fairies were standing in a clearing. When they saw Rachel and Kirsty, they smiled and fluttered their pastel-colored wings.

"These are the other Sweet Fairies," said Monica. "Gabby the Bubble Gum Fairy, Franny the Jelly Bean Fairy, and Shelley the Sugar Fairy."

"What is your job?" asked Rachel.

Monica held out a sparkly pink marshmallow.

"Each of us has a magical treat," said Monica. "We use them to make sure that all the candy in Fairyland and the human world is sweet and delicious."

The other fairies held out their hands, too. Franny had a glittering jelly bean. Gabby was holding a shiny strip of bubble gum, and Shelley had a sparkling packet of popping candy.

"What a wonderful job," said Rachel, gazing around at the brightly colored trees and smiling. "I think this might be

my favorite place in Fairyland."

"Of course, you already know about the Candy Factory orchard," said Shelley. "You know many of our friends."

She waved at a group of fairies who were working at the far end of the orchard.

"It's the Sugar and Spice Fairies with Honey the Candy Fairy and Lizzie the Sweet Treats Fairy," said Kirsty, also waving. "Oh, Monica, thank you so much for bringing us here again."

Thieves in the Orchard

The beautiful Candy Factory trees were chock-full of hard candies, lemon drops, chocolate mints, gummy bears, lollipops, and fudge squares, ready to be picked. Monica fluttered over to a marshmallow tree and plucked a bunch of multicolored marshmallows for Rachel and Kirsty to try.

"It's like eating little puffs of cloud," said Rachel. "They're so incredibly sweet and fluffy."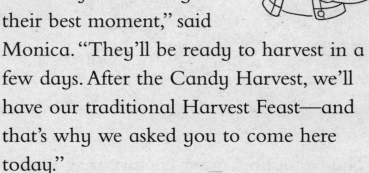

"The treats on the trees are just reaching their best moment," said Monica. "They'll be ready to harvest in a few days. After the Candy Harvest, we'll have our traditional Harvest Feast—and that's why we asked you to come here today."

"We'd all like to invite you to attend the Harvest Feast," said Franny. "Will you come with us?"

"We'd love to," said Kirsty, exchanging an excited grin with Rachel. "It sounds totally amazing."

But then they heard something that

wiped their smiles away.
A horrible cackle echoed
around the orchard, and
Rachel clutched
Kirsty's hand in alarm.

"That sounded like
Jack Frost!" she said.

Suddenly, the Ice
Lord and his goblins
popped out from
behind the trees
around them. They
started shaking the
trees, and candy
began to rain down
around them.

"No, stop!" cried Gabby.
She darted forward, but
the goblins started pelting her

with candy, squawking with laughter when she flew back to the others again.

"Stop throwing those treats!" Jack Frost bellowed at the goblins. "They're mine now—all mine!"

"They're not yours," Monica said bravely. "These treats are meant to be shared by everyone who loves them."

"Fiddlesticks!" Jack Frost retorted. "No one loves candy more than I do. And no one except me is going to get any. I'm opening my own candy shop at the Ice Castle, and only one customer will be allowed. ME!"

Without warning, the goblins charged toward the Sweet Fairies, and the fairies stumbled backward. In their shock, they let go of their magical treats. The goblins caught them and ran back to Jack Frost.

"Honey, Lizzie, help!" called Kirsty. "Sugar and Spice Fairies, help!"

The other fairies zoomed toward them from the opposite end of the orchard.

"You won't catch us!" the goblins squawked nastily.

Jack Frost waved his wand, and there

was a flash of blue lightning and a clap of thunder. Rachel kept her eyes fixed on Jack Frost and saw him shout something, but the noise of the thunder drowned out his voice. Then he and the goblins vanished. Rachel and Kirsty looked around at the half-empty trees as the other fairies reached them.

"They've caused so much damage," said Honey with a groan. "Why does Jack Frost do such horrible things?"

"He hasn't just damaged the trees," said Monica, fluttering over to stand between Rachel and Kirsty. "He's taken our magical treats."

Honey, Lizzie, and the Sugar and Spice Fairies gasped in shock.

"Without them, all candy everywhere will taste horrible," said Lizzie. "Jack Frost must be stopped."

"What are we going to do?" whispered Monica, with tears in her eyes.

"I have an idea," said Rachel. "I saw Jack Frost shout something to the goblins just before he left. I couldn't hear him because of the thunder, but I was trying to read his lips. I'm sure he said

something about the human world. I think he was telling his goblins to go and hide there."

"That's a wonderful clue," said Monica, clasping her hands together. "Rachel and Kirsty, if I come back to your world with you, will you help me look for the goblins?"

The girls agreed right away, and Monica turned to the other fairies.

"As soon as I have news, I will come back," she said. "Now that I have Rachel and Kirsty helping me, I'm sure that we can stop Jack Frost's plans."

She lifted her wand and then swished it through the air. Instantly, the girls were human again and standing in Kirsty's bedroom.

"Where should we start looking?" asked

Monica, fluttering around.

Before the girls could reply, they heard the sound of an engine outside the house. Kirsty dashed to the window.

"It's Aunt Helen," she said. "Monica, my aunt is taking us out for a surprise. Will you come with us? We can keep our eyes peeled for goblins as we go. She works in a candy factory—she might even be taking us there."

"It sounds like a great way to start our search," said Monica.

She dove into Kirsty's pocket to hide, and the girls hurried downstairs to greet Aunt Helen.

Summer Snow

Kirsty threw open the front door and smiled when she saw her fair-haired young aunt.

"Hello, girls!" said Aunt Helen, giving them both a big hug. "I'm thrilled that you can join me for this very special trip. Hurry and get your shoes on—we have a short drive ahead of us."

"Where are we going?" asked Rachel, already filled with excitement.

Aunt Helen's blue eyes shone. "Candy Land is rewarding children in town with candy gift bags for doing good deeds," she said. "The children have been nominated by their families and friends who think that they deserve

a special treat. We've called the program Candy Land's Helping Hands. I thought that you would like to come with me to surprise the first winner."

"That's a wonderful idea," said Kirsty. "I can't wait to see the first winner's face. Who is it?"

"It's a boy named Ori," said Aunt Helen. "He helps at the Tree House Club, which runs camping trips and activities in the woods for younger children."

"I know Ori from school," said Kirsty. "He's really nice."

"He's at the Tree House Club today, getting ready for a camp-out this evening," said Aunt Helen as the girls called good-bye to Mrs. Tate and left the house. "The plan is to surprise him around the campfire with a big bag of marshmallows. They're his favorite candy."

As the girls followed Aunt Helen out to the van, they exchanged an anxious glance with each other. Now that

Monica's magical marshmallow had been stolen, would all marshmallows everywhere taste horrible?

The girls climbed into the back of the van and saw a bulging Candy Land gift bag on the seat. It had pink and white stripes, and *Candy Land's Helping Hands* was written across the side in sparkly silver glitter. As Aunt Helen drove off, Kirsty leaned over and peeked inside.

"Oh no," she whispered.

Rachel peered into the bag and groaned. It should have been full of colorful

marshmallows, but they had all melted into a big, gloopy mess.

"Ori won't enjoy those at all," she said. "We have to find the goblins and get Monica's marshmallow back before he opens the gift bag."

Aunt Helen drove out of the village and through twisty lanes until they came to a wooded area. She parked the van and the girls jumped out, leaving the bag of marshmallows in the van. A young man and woman strode toward them out of the woods.

"Hi, Helen," said the woman. "Who do we have here?"

"I'd like you to meet my niece Kirsty, and her best friend, Rachel," said Aunt Helen. "Girls, Carlotta and Calvin are the leaders of the Tree House Club. They're also old friends of mine from school."

"Not *that* old," said Calvin with a grin.

The three adults laughed and started to talk about their school days. Rachel and Kirsty hovered in the background, not quite sure what to do. Carlotta noticed them and smiled.

"I'm sure you two don't want to listen to us giggling about what we did when we were your age," she said in a kind voice. "Why don't you go and look for Ori? Go along that path and it will take you straight to the tree house. You'll find him and the others there."

She turned back to Calvin and Aunt Helen, and the girls set off along the wooded path that she had pointed out. The girls hurried along, enjoying the sound of twigs cracking under their feet. Birds called to each other, and the scent of pine trees filled the air. The late afternoon sun made a beautiful dappled pattern as it shone through the leaves.

"I love being in the woods," said
Rachel. "You're so lucky to live near a
place like this."

The path wound around to the right,
and the girls saw a huge oak tree with
sprawling branches. Some of the branches
were so big that they were being propped
up by wooden V-shaped crutches. A rope

ladder hung down the trunk, and a group of children was standing there, staring up at the tree house.

"That's Ori," said Kirsty, pointing to the tallest boy.

Ori was wearing a pair of brown shorts and a green T-shirt. The shirt had a picture of a tree on the front and the words *Tree House Club* going around the tree in a circle. He had a clipboard. The other children were younger, but they were wearing the same uniform.

Suddenly, a volley of white balls came flying down from the tree, and the children dodged out of the way. As soon as the balls hit the ground, they fell apart.

"Those look like snowballs," said
Rachel in an astonished voice. "What
are snowballs doing in the forest in the
middle of summer?"

Trouble in the Tree House

Whoosh! A snowball zoomed past Rachel's head and hit the tree behind her. The trunk was suddenly covered in white gloop.

"That's not snow," said Kirsty. "It's marshmallow!"

Dodging through the flying balls of sticky marshmallow, the girls hurried over to Ori.

"Are you OK?" Rachel asked him. "Who could be throwing these things at you?"

"I've been trying to organize the Squirrels for tonight's camp- out," he replied, pointing at the younger  children. "But some misbehaving boys in the tree house keep throwing these sticky, gloopy marshmallows at us. Are you here to help out?"

Rachel and Kirsty didn't know how to

reply. They couldn't lie, but they couldn't tell him the truth, either! Luckily, at that moment, some of the Squirrels started throwing pieces of gooey marshmallow back up at the boys. Soon they were all

covered in the gloopy goo.

"We'll never get everything ready at this rate," Ori said, hanging his head. "I wish those boys would stop it. I've tried to talk to them, but they just keep cackling and squawking at me."

Kirsty and Rachel exchanged a knowing glance.

"Cackling and squawking?" said Rachel. "That sounds like someone we know . . ."

"Ori, try to stop the Squirrels from throwing marshmallows," said Kirsty. "I've got an idea."

She took Rachel's hand and pulled her deeper into the woods until they reached a grassy clearing. Monica fluttered out of Kirsty's pocket.

"I heard everything," she said. "You

think that they're goblins, don't you?"

"Yes," said Rachel. "And we have to get up to that tree house."

Monica waved her wand, and suddenly the woods seemed much bigger. Rachel and Kirsty were still standing in the clearing, but now the grass seemed as tall

as pine trees.

"We're fairies again," said Kirsty, twirling around and fluttering her wings in delight. "Now we can easily check on the boys in the tree house."

"Let's be quick," said Rachel. "If they are goblins, they're sure to think of a new

way to make trouble soon."

Together, the three fairies rose into the air and zoomed toward the tree house, dodging the marshmallows that were flying around them. Kirsty was first.

"There are four windows," she called out. "I can see goblins in three of them."

"Fly toward the fourth window," Monica called. "We can't let the goblins see us."

They flew in single file and rose high into the air, and then swooped down to the fourth window. Hovering there, they could see three goblins in the other windows. The goblins were busy throwing gloopy marshmallow

balls down at the children as fast as they could.

The long-nosed goblin in the middle window had a huge bucket of gloop beside him. All the goblins were plunging their hands into it to make their marshmallow balls. As the fairies watched, the bucket ran out of gloop.

"I'll try to fill it again," said the long-nosed goblin.

He waved a pink marshmallow over the bucket, and it was instantly full again.

"That's my magical marshmallow," said Monica with a gasp. "We've found it!"

Monica's marshmallow looked more delicious than any marshmallow Rachel and Kirsty had ever seen. It had a magical sparkle, and it was perfectly squishy and round.

"Why are the goblins throwing the marshmallow gloop instead of eating it?" Rachel asked. "It's unlike them—they're usually so greedy."

"Goblins only like bogmallows," said Monica. "They're like marshmallows, but green and slimy. They're very smelly.

But goblins love them."

Just then, a gloopy marshmallow
ball hurtled toward Rachel and Kirsty.
They leaned away from each other, and
it passed between them. When Kirsty
looked at Rachel, she saw her best
friend's eyes sparkling.

"I have an idea," she said with an
excited grin. "If the goblins want a
marshmallow fight so much, maybe we
should let them have one."

The three fairies slipped into the tree
house and each of them scooped up
a handful of marshmallow gloop.
Staying in the shadows, each of them
aimed at a different goblin. Kirsty held
up three fingers and counted down.
Three, two, one, fire!

Each goblin was hit by marshmallow at

exactly the same moment. They all spun
around and glared at each other.

"Hey!" squawked one.

"Stop that!" squealed the goblin with
the long nose.

"You'll be sorry!" the
third shouted.

The goblins started
hurling handfuls of
marshmallow gloop
at each other, and

squealing as they were hit. The goblin with the long nose was still clutching the magical marshmallow in his hand.

"I'll get it!" Rachel exclaimed.

She swooped toward the goblin, hoping to pluck the marshmallow out of his hand. She stretched out her arm, ready to take the magical treat. But just before she reached him, the long-nosed goblin looked up and saw her.

"Buzz off, you pesky fairy," he yelled. "It's mine!"

He waved the magical marshmallow over the bucket.

"It doesn't belong to you," said Rachel in a gentle voice, hovering in front of him.

"But I need it," wailed the goblin. "I want bogmallows now!"

Smelly Sweets

Monica beckoned Rachel back to her.

"That's what he really wants," she whispered. "Bogmallows! He is trying to use my magical marshmallow to make slimy, smelly bogmallows, but that's not what the magical marshmallow is for. That's why they're coming out so strange and gloopy."

"We can't get the magical marshmallow back like this," said Kirsty. "Monica, can you turn us back into humans again? I have an idea."

The three fairies flew back into the woods and landed in the clearing. Then Monica waved her wand and turned Rachel and Kirsty back into humans again.

"Thank you, Monica," said Kirsty. "I know that you need your magical marshmallow to make tasty treats,

44

but do you have enough magic to make
a big bowl of bogmallows?"

"Certainly," said Monica. "With
bogmallows, the worse they taste, the
more the goblins like them."

She tapped a nearby log with her
wand three times,
and a large
bowl of green
bogmallows
appeared in
front of them.
The smell was
terrible, and a
faint green
mist hovered
over the bowl.
Rachel and
Kirsty held their noses.

"Ugh, it's like rotten eggs and mold and unwashed socks," said Rachel. "How can the goblins *like* them?"

"I don't know," said Kirsty. "But they do—and that might give us a way to get the magical marshmallow back."

Monica slipped back into Kirsty's pocket, and then the girls made their way back to the tree house with the smelly bogmallows. Ori and the younger children saw them coming, but staggered backward when they smelled the stench of the bogmallows.

"What is that?" Ori exclaimed,

covering his nose and mouth.

"We have a way to stop those boys," said Rachel. "Trust us."

Ori nodded, and watched as Rachel and Kirsty climbed up the rope ladder with the bogmallow bowl. Before they reached the top, the goblins had already smelled the bogmallows. They were leaning out over the rope ladder, licking their lips.

"Give them to us," said the long-nosed goblin as soon as the girls were in the tree house.

"We'd love to," said Kirsty. "All

we want in return
is that marshmallow
you're holding in
your hand."

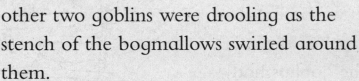

The goblin
glanced down
at the sparkling
magical treat. The
other two goblins were drooling as the
stench of the bogmallows swirled around
them.

"Jack Frost wouldn't like it . . ." said the
long-nosed goblin.

"Jack Frost isn't here," said the second
goblin in an irritated voice. "But a
yummy bowl of bogmallows is here, and
I want them in my tummy. So hand over
the silly fairy's candy, and let's feast!"

The long-nosed goblin couldn't

resist any longer. He shoved the pink marshmallow into Kirsty's hand, and snatched the bowl away from her.

"BOGMALLOWS!" boomed the three goblins, scooping the green, smelly candy into their mouths. "YUMMY!"

Monica zoomed out of Kirsty's pocket, and Kirsty handed her the magical marshmallow. It immediately shrank down to fairy size.

"This is wonderful!" said Monica, twirling around in midair. "Now I can make sure that marshmallows all around the world taste absolutely perfect."

"Jack Frost is going to be very angry," said the long-nosed goblin, who had globs of bogmallow flying out of his mouth as he talked. "But these are so delicious that I just don't care."

"Kirsty, let's go back to the van and check Ori's marshmallows," said Rachel in an urgent voice. "We have to make

sure that they are back
to normal."

Monica hid in
Kirsty's pocket
again, and the
girls hurried
down the rope
ladder. Ori
was already
organizing
the Squirrels
and helping
them clean the
marshmallow
goo off their
uniforms.

"Thank you
for stopping those
terrible boys,"

he called out to Rachel and Kirsty.

"No problem," Rachel called to him. "We'll be back in a minute."

The girls ran back down the path through the woods until they reached the place where Aunt Helen was still chatting with Carlotta and Calvin. Panting, they darted over to the van, opened the back door, and peered into the pink-and-white-striped bag. It was full of fluffy, yummy-looking marshmallows.

"They look perfect," said Kirsty, heaving a huge sigh of relief. "Thank goodness. Now everything is ready for a wonderful Candy Land surprise."

Just then, Aunt Helen turned around and noticed them.

"Hello, girls," she said with a laugh. "Have you come back to check on us? I'm sorry we didn't catch up with you— we got distracted talking about our memories from school.

53

Are Ori and the Squirrels ready for the camp-out?"

"I hope so," said Kirsty, smiling. "These marshmallows look amazing—and ready to be eaten!"

Helping Hands

When dusk fell, Aunt Helen and the
girls were hiding behind the big oak
tree. Aunt Helen was holding the bag
of marshmallows in her arms. Carlotta,
Calvin, and Ori were sitting around the
campfire with the Squirrels. They sang the
Tree House Club song, and then passed
around mugs of frothy hot chocolate.

"This is wonderful," said Ori. "It's exactly what I love best about the Tree House Club."

"There's just one thing missing," said Carlotta, winking at Calvin.

"There sure is," said Calvin.

Rachel, Kirsty, and Aunt Helen stepped out from behind the big oak tree and walked into the light of the campfire.

"Hello," said Ori. "I wondered where you disappeared to earlier."

"We didn't go far," said Kirsty.

"We've come back because of you," said Rachel, smiling.

Ori looked around at his friends, and they all smiled at him.

"Ori, your friends think you are a very special person," said Aunt Helen. "They have all voted for you to be the first winner of Candy Land's Helping Hands award. Congratulations! Here is your prize."

She handed the bag to Ori, who gasped in delight when he peeked inside.

"My favorite!" he said, turning pink with pleasure. "Thank you."

"Thank you for all your help with the Squirrels and the Tree House Club," said Calvin, shaking his hand.

Rachel nudged Kirsty and pointed at the oak tree. The three goblins had come down the rope ladder and were watching, still stuffing bogmallows into their mouths.

"I'd like to share these with everyone," said Ori, passing the bag around the group of excited Squirrels.

"We can toast them over the fire for you," said Carlotta.

The Squirrels cheered, and Ori noticed the goblins standing nearby.

"You can have some, too, if you'd like," he said. "There's enough for everyone."

The goblins were still in their Tree House Club uniforms, so Ori thought they were ordinary boys.

"We already have some," squawked the long-nosed goblin awkwardly. "But . . . um . . . thanks."

They came and joined the group around the fire. A few of the Squirrels moved away from the smell of the

bogmallows, but they still made the
goblins feel welcome.

"It's nice to see the goblins enjoying
themselves," said Kirsty in a low voice.
"That's another good deed that Ori's
done for others."

Dusk had passed now, and night had
fallen. The moon was shining brightly,
giving the tree house a soft glow.

"The tree house looks almost magical, doesn't it?" said Aunt Helen, noticing the girls staring at it.

Rachel and Kirsty exchanged a secret smile.

"May we go up to the top, Aunt Helen?" Kirsty asked.

"Yes, as long as you're careful," said Aunt Helen.

Once again, the girls climbed up the swinging rope ladder to the tree house. It was even more exciting to be up there in the moonlight. As soon as they were inside, Monica flew out of Rachel's pocket.

"Thank you both so

much for your help," she said. "I'm glad I stayed long enough to see Ori get his award. I want to give you both a treat, too—something to say thank you for all you have done."

She waved her wand and a bowl of fluffy marshmallows appeared on the tree house floor. Monica hovered above the bowl, and the moonlight made her wings glimmer.

"Pick up a marshmallow," she said, smiling. "I'm going to show you how to make taffy."

Monica showed the girls how to twist the marshmallows using just their fingertips, and then pull them apart.

"Now press them together, and twist and pull again," said Monica. "Keep going."

Slowly, the mixture stopped coming apart. It stretched between their fingers, a soft and glossy new type of candy.

"This is fun," said Rachel, giggling as she watched the marshmallows change.

"Fun *and* delicious," said Monica. "I
hope you enjoy eating it. Thank you
again. I must return to Fairyland."

"Please tell the other Sweet Fairies
that they can count on us," said Kirsty.
Rachel nodded.

Monica smiled, and then she was
gone in a puff of
silvery fairy
dust. Rachel
and Kirsty
popped
pieces
of taffy
into their
mouths and
shared a hug.

"I'm so glad
that we could help

Monica get her magical marshmallow back from Jack Frost and the goblins," said Rachel. "I just hope that we can help the other Sweet Fairies, too."

"We can't let Jack Frost ruin the rest of the Candy Land's Helping Hands treats," said Kirsty. "And we won't let the Harvest Feast be a disaster, either."

"Then we have more magical adventures ahead," said Rachel with a sparkle in her eyes. "It's going to be an exciting week!"

RAINBOW magic
THE SWEET FAIRIES

Rachel and Kirsty have found Monica's
missing magical item.
Now it's time for them to help

Gabby
the Bubble Gum Fairy!

Join their next adventure in
this special sneak peek . . .

The Playground Buddy

Rachel Walker whizzed down the candy-
cane slide. She squealed with laughter
as she zoomed off the end onto a
trampoline and bounced into the air.

"This is the best park in the whole
wide world," she called happily to her
best friend, Kirsty Tate, who was sitting
at the top of the slide.

"WHEEEEEE!" Kirsty sang out as she
shot down the slide and bounced down
beside Rachel. "It's so much fun. I'm so
glad that Aunt Helen asked us both to
meet her here."

Rachel was staying with Kirsty for a whole week. It was always fun visiting Wetherbury, but this time it was extra exciting. Kirsty's aunt Helen, who worked at Candy Land, a candy factory, had asked the girls to help her with some very special deliveries. Candy Land was giving out Helping Hands awards for people who were doing wonderful things to help the community. It was part of Aunt Helen's job to present the winners with bags of their favorite candy, and Rachel and Kirsty were proud to help.

"Your aunt Helen should be here soon," said Rachel, checking her watch.

The girls stopped bouncing and looked over at the factory. The candy-themed park was on the beautiful grounds of the factory, on the outskirts of Wetherbury.

The tall slide looked as if it had been made from candy canes, the swings were shaped like jelly beans, and the merry-go-round looked like a big cookie. On the far side of the park, some boys were playing by a fence that seemed to be made of strawberry licorice laces.

RAINBOW magic

Which Magical Fairies Have You Met?

- ❏ The Rainbow Fairies
- ❏ The Weather Fairies
- ❏ The Jewel Fairies
- ❏ The Pet Fairies
- ❏ The Sports Fairies
- ❏ The Ocean Fairies
- ❏ The Princess Fairies
- ❏ The Superstar Fairies
- ❏ The Fashion Fairies
- ❏ The Sugar & Spice Fairies
- ❏ The Earth Fairies
- ❏ The Magical Crafts Fairies
- ❏ The Baby Animal Rescue Fairies
- ❏ The Fairy Tale Fairies
- ❏ The School Day Fairies
- ❏ The Storybook Fairies
- ❏ The Friendship Fairies

SCHOLASTIC

HIT entertainment

Find all of your favorite fairy friends at
scholastic.com/rainbowmagic

RMFAIRY17

SPECIAL EDITION

Which Magical Fairies Have You Met?

- ❏ Joy the Summer Vacation Fairy
- ❏ Holly the Christmas Fairy
- ❏ Kylie the Carnival Fairy
- ❏ Stella the Star Fairy
- ❏ Shannon the Ocean Fairy
- ❏ Trixie the Halloween Fairy
- ❏ Gabriella the Snow Kingdom Fairy
- ❏ Juliet the Valentine Fairy
- ❏ Mia the Bridesmaid Fairy
- ❏ Flora the Dress-Up Fairy
- ❏ Paige the Christmas Play Fairy
- ❏ Emma the Easter Fairy
- ❏ Cara the Camp Fairy
- ❏ Destiny the Rock Star Fairy
- ❏ Belle the Birthday Fairy
- ❏ Olympia the Games Fairy
- ❏ Selena the Sleepover Fairy

- ❏ Cheryl the Christmas Tree Fairy
- ❏ Florence the Friendship Fairy
- ❏ Lindsay the Luck Fairy
- ❏ Brianna the Tooth Fairy
- ❏ Autumn the Falling Leaves Fairy
- ❏ Keira the Movie Star Fairy
- ❏ Addison the April Fool's Day Fairy
- ❏ Bailey the Babysitter Fairy
- ❏ Natalie the Christmas Stocking Fairy
- ❏ Lila and Myla the Twins Fairies
- ❏ Chelsea the Congratulations Fairy
- ❏ Carly the School Fairy
- ❏ Angelica the Angel Fairy
- ❏ Blossom the Flower Girl Fairy
- ❏ Skyler the Fireworks Fairy
- ❏ Giselle the Christmas Ballet Fairy
- ❏ Alicia the Snow Queen Fairy

■ SCHOLASTIC

Find all of your favorite fairy friends at
scholastic.com/rainbowmagic

3 stories in each one!

HIT entertainment

RMSPECIAL20